Return
of the Maneater

by

Anuj Sabharwal

Return of the Maneater

by Anuj Sabharwal

ISBN: 978-93-62766-12-0

Published by

DOUBLE 9 BOOKS

2/13-B, Ansari Road
Daryaganj, New Delhi – 110002
info@double9books.com
www.double9books.com
Tel. 011-40042856

ABOUT THE AUTHOR

Born and brought up in Delhi, Anuj studied English Literature at Delhi University and did software program from NIIT. He worked with American Multinationals like eFunds and FIS Global, and for an American Express process. Anuj turned to writing as a career in 2013. He has written columns for an online magazine, 'The Indian Economist.' He writes on social issues. His other books are November Rain, Little Arnie, Revenge of a maneater, Gazala and Lala Khatri. All books are available on Amazon. November Rain is a story of Anglo-Indian girl Ashley Coleman who goes on life changing journey to find the truth behind torrid times that she faced. Little Arnie is a story of young kid who has been abandoned by his mother. He grows and turns into a teenager with the love and care of his relatives and neighbours. Revenge of a maneater is about revenge taken by Sherkhan who follows, stalks and terrorize Khan, an engineer who had shot his girlfriend tigress. Gazala is about Professor Aditya Raj Khanna who falls in love with his student Gazala. Lala Khatri is a partition story. His next book, Return of the Maneater is about Sherkhan.

CONTENTS

Foreword

The people of the Indian subcontinent, primarily British India believed that tigers possessed supernatural powers. Much of folklore narrates tales of terrifying man-eaters. A strange aura surrounds these tales. A tiger that is born and grows up in the wild never considers mortal beings as their legitimate prey. It is only when tigers have been incapacitated through wounds or old age; they are compelled to take to a diet of human flesh. The man-eaters were regarded as enraged or malevolent deities (or spirits or demons), and ghosts of their victims ride on them to direct them to the following prey. The brutes were tamed devilish, and the villagers did not dare to utter 'Bagh' for the fear of it. Such fear of man-eaters was not unique in British India, and it existed even in Africa. The two ferocious lions of Tsavo were considered Devils by the labourers who worked on the rail track. Tsavo became a hazardous place to live. They were recognized as 'The Ghost and the Darkness.' The man-eaters owned the day and the night. They seemed to possess highly developed collaborative hunting techniques unknown to the species. The killed without fear and a reason. A few called them the spirits of village elders who wanted to end the reign of while men in the world. Whatever they endure, the lions endure absolute evils. The duo settled for over a hundred victims between them before Colonel John Patterson ended their reign of terror. Wherever tigers and lions have roamed, we find intriguing tales. This book contains such a tale of Sherkhan.

Numerous readers possess a voracious appetite for diversity, profound sentiments, and thrilling escapades. The composition of this literary work has been tailored specifically to cater to such readers.

Preface

Save the tiger, save the pride!

The shots that wound a tiger seriously turn it into a ferocious man-eater. This vicious man-eater usually stalks lonely travellers on forest roads and prowls isolated villages. The villagers cower inside their huts for days and wait for the righteous saviour to end the terror. Khan, an engineer did not wound a tiger. He shot the man-eating tigress and girlfriend of Sherkhan to help the villager, Nawab. Sherkhan was also a man-eater and thrived on humans. He watched Khan and Nawab. It was never heard of in history of the mankind that the man-eating tiger followed a human to take revenge. Sherkhan followed, stalked and terrorized Khan. Sherkhan subsequently became a subject of great interest after he took his revenge. Many wondered and were curious if Sherkhan persisted in his carnivorous tendencies, acquired a new mate, or continued to stalk humans after exacting his revenge. The book 'Return of the Maneater' answers all.

Acknowledgements

I wish to thank Him.

Sherkhan, a tiger known for preying on humans, sought revenge against Khan for the killing of his tigress. With relentless determination, Sherkhan pursued Khan until he successfully exacted his revenge. This act has left many in awe of Sherkhan's unwavering resolve and ferocious nature. If Khan had refrained from venturing into the treacherous jungle in search of Gangu's cow, he could have easily avoided a dangerous encounter with the notorious Sherkhan. Similarly, had Khan chosen not to shoot the tigress that was playing with the tiger, he could have effortlessly avoided the confrontation with Sherkhan. Prior to these events, Sherkhan was unfamiliar to Khan, who would not have believed that a tiger would relentlessly pursue and hunt him down if someone had warned him. Initially skeptical, I was told a chilling tale of Sherkhan's revenge by Banke. Before returning home, I had the opportunity to spend a few days in Jim Corbett Park, the very location where the incident took place. However, one question lingered in my mind: What became of Sherkhan? Did he alter his behavior and ceased consuming human flesh? Did he find a new girlfriend and lived happily with her or they continued to hunt together? Banke contacted me after a month..

'Sir, I have some news to share with you!' Banke said.

'It's good Banke that you called. Even I wanted to talk,'

'Would you believe that a few man-eating tigers are roaming around Corbett Park?'

'Yes, I heard about them. Could you please provide more details?'

'It's a ferocious pair, hunting down men even in broad daylight,'

'Oh! That's what Sherkhan did many years ago. Did Sherkhan return with his another girlfriend? Haa…' I joked.

'No, sir. These tigers are different! They are selecting their victims from the highway,' Banke clarified.

'It's unusual! The only tiger to do so was the Sunderkhal maneater,'

'Sir! It is langdi and her paramour! They are hunting in Mohaan,' Banke informed.

'Umm… Mohaan! Is it not a rather bustling location?'

'Indeed, sir,' Banke confirmed. 'The area boasts numerous resorts, a thriving market, and even a college. The locals are understandably quite frightened.'

'Well, it is no surprise,' I remarked.

'Man-eaters have no qualms about attacking humans. They are, after all, vulnerable to them.'

'Sir, I request you to consider visiting the area and learning more about these creatures,' Banke suggested.

'It would be quite an exhilarating experience, and you may even uncover a fascinating story.'

'I must respectfully decline,' I replied with a smile. 'It would be unwise to venture into the territory of man-eating animals without proper protection, solely for the sake of a story.'

Banke suggested that one need not traverse Mohaan to acquire a story, as the locals are willing to share their experiences. Many have witnessed hunting on the highway, and one may sit by a bonfire on a chilly night to hear their tales.

'I am curious about Sherkhan. Could you enlighten me on what happened to him?' I inquired.

Banke chuckled hysterically and replied, 'It appears that Sherkhan has captured your attention, Sahib.'

'Please do tell me more about Sherkhan.'

Banke obliged, 'My grandfather used to recount stories of Sherkhan. He was a ferocious maneater, yet equally cunning. Even after he had hunted down Khan, he continued to terrorize people and even hunted many hunters.'

'Oh! It's chilling to think about how Sherkhan hunted hunters without them realizing it,'

'Sherkhan always executed his actions with a well-thought-out strategy, unknown to the hunters,'

'Did Sherkhan devise plans?'

'Indeed, he intelligently strategized against Khan and other hunters, becoming increasingly astute and cunning.'

I found it challenging to resist delving further into the subject of Sherkhan. Consequently, following some initial hesitation, I ultimately agreed to Banke's proposition.

'Okay, I shall visit you in a few days,'

'Sahib, I sense Sherkhan's presence in the jungle. I believe his spirit still wanders within Corbett Park,'

'Exercise caution, as he may have a scheme in store for you!' I laughed unaware of what was to come.

During my recent stay at Dhikala, I once again booked a room. At night, Banke joined me and we gathered around a bonfire to discuss the infamous Mohaan man-eaters and, in particular, Sherkhan. As we chatted, the deer clan grazed in the background, unaware that some of them would soon become prey for carnivores.

'Sir,' Banke exclaimed excitedly, 'a tiger attacked a contractor near the Dhangari gate. The guards witnessed the tiger devouring its prey as he returned from Dhikala.'

'Did it happen during the day?' Curious, I asked.

'Yes, it was in full view at noon!' Banke replied.

'Poor guy,' I exclaimed, raising my hands in disgust.

'It was a fully grown tiger and he ate the contractor fully,'

'I am confident that the guards have received sufficient training to cope with it,'

'Yes! They see tigers every other day. But, this was different,'

'Maneater hardly strikes its meal in daylight!'

'It was a young, handsome, and fully grown tiger,'

'But, you mentioned a couple who have made Mohaan their hunting ground,'

'Dhangarhi gate is only a few miles from Mohaan. The tigers travel quickly!'

'What about the other incident?'

'It was an unbelievable hunt, something that never happened in Corbett Park,'

'Umm... go on...please continue,'

'The tigress jumped on the boys who were returning after a day picnic in Ranikhet. She had seen them from a distance and positioned herself accordingly,' Banke explained.

'Was it still daylight?' I inquired.

'No, the light was beginning to fade when tigress waited for them at the bend. When they slowed down, the tigress pounced and took away the boy who was sitting at the back.' Banke said, shaking his head.

'The strategy employed was reminiscent of her forebears, involving concealment behind foliage followed by assault upon unsuspecting individuals. Uff… the poor guys!'

'She ate the victim fully. However, there was no male tiger with her.'

'How do you know?'

'There was another boy who fell down when tigress pounced. He ran away in the opposite direction towards Mohaan and alarmed the policemen. He never mentioned another tiger,'

'I admire the brave guy who didn't shun his senses!'

'The meal was finished quickly. I suspect there was a male tiger somewhere in the bush,'

'The young guy escaped because the male tiger didn't follow him.'

'Who was the other victim?'

'He was a lonely traveler walking alone on Mohaan highway. He was not fully consumed.'

'Do you have any idea what made them man eaters?'

'I spoke with the villager, who informed me that the tigress is likely handicapped with a leg problem,'

'What about the male?'

'It is possible that he may have been influenced by the female tiger's interactions with humans and adopted her behaviors,'

'Do you know of any other incident?'

'Yes, the male tiger pounced on the forest guard who was returning from Sarpdulli.'

'Was he eaten fully?'

'No, he only sustained injuries. The other guards who were accompanying him managed to rescue him,'

'Oh! They managed to snatch the prey away from the tiger. He must be quite enraged,'

'What frustrates me is that the news of these man eaters does not receive significant attention, and we are left to face this struggle alone,' Banke sighed.

'What's the latest on them?'

'Langdi has been caught. The tests proved her to be a man-eater. However, the male tiger is still at large!'

'Do they have cubs?'

'I have no news on it!'

'Man-eaters are cunning! The male tiger must have escaped into the forest.'

A loud call from the tiger dispersed the deer. The drops of sweat were visible on my cheeks. Banke noticed it and smiled at me. I smiled back nervously.

'Sahib, I hope the male leaves man-eating habits and returns to his normal food.'

'Only the tiger knows his preference,'

'He still prefers humans. Recently he took a middle-aged man from Dhangarhi nallah. He was partying with his friends,'

'Engaging in revelry with acquaintances in the forest was an imprudent choice. Were they drinking?' I raised my eyebrow.

'I am unaware of the exact circumstances, however, it was evident that the individuals in question were engaging in boisterous behavior and dancing. The tiger, perceiving their presence, became aware of their activities. Subsequently, the man proceeded to attend to his personal needs, only to find himself unexpectedly ensnared by the formidable creature,'

'I feel sad for him. Umm...Banke! What did Sherkhan prefer after Khan?'

'I anticipated that you would bring this up.'

'I am quite intrigued!'

'Well, we can delve into it after our meal. I am starving, just like Sherkhan!' Banke patted his thighs and grinned.

The dinner was served, and Banke thoroughly enjoyed the meal. Personally, I prefer to have a lighter dinner.

'What exactly happened after Khan had been slain?'

'When Khan didn't report at the dam, a few laborers decided to visit the rest house,' Banke said.

'Were they aware of Sherkhan?'

'Who wasn't, Sahib? The ferocious tiger had terrorized whole of Ramnagar, Marchula, and Kalagarh!'

'Hmm…' I nodded in agreement.

'They had sticks, lanterns, and drums with them. They reached safely and rescued my grandpa,'

'Your grandpa must have been in a miserable condition,'

'Yes, he was hungry, exhausted, and drenched in sweat when they found him. Spending the night alone in the rest house was quite a challenge,'

'Undoubtedly, witnessing Sherkhan devouring Khan must have been a harrowing experience,'

'I do not believe that he made any attempt to look out of the window. He informed the laborers that he had locked himself in the bedroom and waited,'

'Indeed! Just a few hours ago, they were confined together in the rest house!' I exclaimed, shaking my head in disbelief.

'Bhoora and Bhoori provided comfort to my grandfather. They offered him water and served him food,'

'Who were they?'

'They were laborers employed at the dam. They were engaged to be married and resided near our village.'

'I can only imagine the condition your grandpa must have been. Nobody deserves this!'

'Indeed, no one should bear witness to what my grandfather endured.'

'Did they take your grandpa back to the village?' I inquired.

'No, they took him to the dam. They had a camp there!'

'It was a wise decision. Sherkhan would have visited the rest house for Grandpa,'

'I can't say about that. We would never know. But, Sherkhan continued his fury against humans. He sought revenge relentlessly!'

'May I inquire as to the intended meaning of your statement? Did he not seek retribution against Khan?'

'No, he wasn't finished. He persisted in his consumption of human flesh, driven by a deep-seated animosity and antipathy towards mankind.'

'This is the reason I am here. I want to understand what happened with him,'

'Sherkhan was uncontrollable and nobody dared to hunt him,'

'I would not have attempted to enter the forest where Sherkhan roamed. It must have required immense bravery for those who labored and resided alongside Sherkhan.'

'Undoubtedly, their act of rescuing my grandfather was an act of great courage.' Banke nodded his head.

Gangu was locked in the bedroom, petrified by the menacing growls of Sherkhan, who was devouring Khan. Although Gangu was thirsty, his fear was too great and he knew there was no chance of help. Cunningly, Sherkhan slyly eyed the forest rest house's main door, seemingly aware of Gangu's presence. Suddenly, Sherkhan moved towards the door and growled fiercely, causing Gangu to shiver. The next morning, the forest was calm and Sherkhan had eaten Khan and moved away without making any noise or looking at the main door. In the afternoon, Gangu heard the voices of laborers who had come to find Khan, who had not shown up at the dam.

'There is a conspicuous absence of any activity in this vicinity. It appears that Khan Sahib has yet to make his presence known,' Bhoora said.

'Yes, no sign of caretaker either,' Bhoori nodded in agreement.

'O Hariya! Hariya!' shouted Prakash, the laborer.

'Where are you, hopeless man?' shouted Bhoora.

The group looked at each other in surprise when they saw Gangu at the main door. His eyes were filled with fear and his complexion appeared pallid. Upon spotting the laborers and assistance, he emitted a loud and frantic cry.

'Gangu! What are you doing here?' asked Prakash.

'You were supposed to be at the village. What brought you here?' Bhoora asked.

He assumed a seated position, resting on his haunches, and lowered his countenance. Sensing his anguish, Bhoori urgently suggested providing him with some water.

Prakash offered the water, which Gangu drank thirstily and returned the pot, still crying.

'What's wrong Gangu? Why are you crying? And why you were locked in the rest house?" asked Prakash who was concerned. He placed his hand on Gangu's shoulders.

Gangu refrained from uttering any words and instead gestured towards the well. Consequently, all individuals present directed their gaze towards the well, their expressions reflecting a sense of perplexity and uncertainty.

'Bhoola, why don't you go there and see what is Gangu referring to?' said Bhoori.

Bhoola, perplexed, glanced at Prakash and the others. He cautiously approached the well, taking measured steps. Prakash discerned a sense of trepidation in Gangu's gaze. 'Wait for me!' Prakash cautioned.

Prakash and Bhoora observed the presence of paw prints in close proximity to the well, exchanging apprehensive looks.

'It appears that baagh has been present in this vicinity,' whispered Prakash.

'This is the cause for Gangu's distress," stated Bhoora. He glanced back at Gangu, who was still weeping. Bhoori observed Bhoora with a mixture of curiosity and composure.

'Be careful! Keep the stick ready!' Prakash pointed to Bhoora.

'Do you believe it will be effective?'

'No, it won't!' Prakash shook his head frantically.

'The gun!' Prakash pointed towards the well.

'The bones!' Bhoora pointed near the canvas bag. He shouted loudly.

Bhoori and Arif ran over to join them, while Champa, Jumman and others stayed near Gangu, who had calmed down slightly.

'Argh…' Bhoori tried to say but the words choked.

'It appears as though the tiger had a feast!'Arif remarked.

Prakash, with a look of astonishment, inquired, 'On whom?'

'It is no surprise that Gangu was trembling,' said Bhoora.

'Gangu has an answer to it!' Arif looked at Prakash.

'The tiger consumed its prey entirely,' said Bhoora.

'Let's go to Gangu and ask him about it,' suggested Prakash.

Bhoora surveyed the surrounding forest, but there was no indication of the tiger's presence.

'Remain here whilst we inquire of Gangu,' Prakash directed, gesturing towards Arif.

'I won't for a bag full of money!' Arif refused.

'It doesn't matter. The man has been cleaned.' Bhoora said.

Gangu was still squatting and gasping for air. Occasionally, he lifted his hands and pointed towards the well.

'Gangu! What happened here? Who was the man? What you were doing in the rest house?' Prakash inquired.

Gangu remained silent and cried loudly.

'Gangu, look at me! Baagh has gone. There is no danger now. You are safe!' Bhoora tried to comfort Gangu.

'It might come back...' Gangu finally answered.

'Who might come back?' asked Bhoori.

'Sherkhan!' Gangu replied.

Bhoora exclaimed with astonishment, 'Sherkhan, the notorious predator! Is he responsible for this?'

'But, why did he eat the man? What prompted your presence here?' asked Prakash.

'Sherkhan and his girlfriend were hunting for months. They were ferocious! Did they kill the man?' Bhoora inquired further.

'Khan Sahib shot Baagh's girilfriend. Subsequently, Sherkhan pursued us.' answered Gangu.

'What? Khan Sahib! He was employed to work at the dam. The English gentleman is eagerly awaiting his arrival!' exclaimed Prakash, widening his eyes in astonishment.

'The wait is over!' chuckled Jumman.

'Why did Khan Sahib shoot the tigress?' asked Bhoora.

'Khan Sahib was en route to the dam. For a night he stayed at my hut. The following morning, I requested his assistance in locating my missing cow, which had strayed into the wilderness,' elucidated Gangu

'But, why you sought his aid in searching for a cow?' Prakash queried, his eyebrow raised in curiosity.

'We had been residing in seclusion due to the presence of Sherkhan and his partner, resulting in a lack of sustenance and resources, including fodder for the cow,'

'We all had been living behind closed doors after the sunset!' sighed Prakash.

Bhoora expressed his frustration by exclaiming, 'Oh Gangu! You have sacrificed Khan Sahib!'

Gangu clarified, 'I did not sacrifice Khan Sahib. I merely requested Sahib to shoot Sherkhan. However, he mistakenly shot the tigress instead.'

Bhoora was taken aback and questioned, 'This is unbelievable! Why did he shoot the tigress?'

'I had taken refuge in the expansive tree concealed behind the large leaves. Sahib had instructed me to ascend it,'

Prakash inquired, 'And where was Sahib at the time?'

'He was situated on the adjacent tree, in close proximity to the stream where the tigers were frolicking,'

Prakash deduced, 'So, it appears that the tigers did not pose a threat to either you or Khan Sahib.'

'Yes, but they had killed my cow!' Gangu raised voice.

'It was an unprovoked shot,' Bhoora sympathized.

'Regardless, they had killed the cow. Khan Sahib took the shot at my request,'

'Why did you ask him to shoot?' asked Prakash.

'I desired to eliminate them. They have caused chaos in our lives!' retorted Gangu with anger.

'What about Sherkhan?'Bhoora inquired.

'He ran into the forest! My cow…' Gangu cried and was clearly upset.

Bhoori suggested, 'Grant him some leniency, as he is distraught.'

'Give him a bite and some water,' said Prakash.

Bhoora, Prakash, and other sat around Gangu on their haunches, offering support. In her quest for reassurance, Bhoori involuntarily cast a glance over her shoulder, hoping to catch a glimpse of Sherkhan.

'Bhoori, he has absconded!' Bhoora declared, accompanied by a smile.

'Someone should promptly inform Mr. Cook at the dam about the current situation,' Prakash suggested.

'Yes, the English gentleman must be eagerly awaiting us!' said Bhoori.

'And for Khan Sahib!' said Bhoora.

'Who exactly is Mr. Cook?" Gangu inquired while taking a sip of water?'

'Khan Sahib was supposed to collaborate with Mr. Cook. He is a highly experienced engineer stationed at the dam!' explained Prakash.

'He has camped near the dam with his wife!' said Bhoora.

'Jumman! Please get back to the dam and bring Sahib here!'

'Can't Gangu walk back with us to the dam?'

'No, he is not fit enough to walk. He is in bad shape emotionally,' said Prakash.

'I am afraid of Sherkhan. I won't go back alone!' Jumman shrugged. He expressed fear.

'Let him stay here. I will go with Bhoora!' said Bhoori.

'Yes, it's a wise suggestion,' smiled Jumman.

'Don't call yourself a man, Jumman!' Prakash taunted.

'Be cautious! Take a stick with you,' suggested Gangu. He seemed to have gathered himself a little.

'Hmm...' Bhoora nodded.

'Let's take Gangu to the room and lock ourselves. Bhoora will take some time. Sherkhan may return, as he is aware of Gangu's presence!'

'What is the status of Hariya's return? Should he come back, what would be the course of action?'

'It appears that Sherkhan has prevailed over him, as he has been absent for two days.'

'Indeed, we must expedite our return before Sherkhan does so...' Gangu's countenance fell, and Prakash discerned a sense of trepidation in his gaze.

'We should have brought Shera with us. He would have scented the baagh,' said Bhoori.

'Rather, we should have borrowed the gun from Cook sahib,' suggested Bhoora.

'What would the stick do in front of Sherkhan?' Bhoori shrugged.

'I refuse to be defeated by any tiger,' Bhoora proudly stroked his mustache.

'Sherkhan is not just any tiger. He possesses cunning ferocity, and poses a significant threat! He could be lurking behind any bush,' suggested Bhoori.

'Whatever…uhh,'

'What if Sherkhan were to appear? How would you ensure my protection?'

'I would offer myself!' said Bhoora.

'Absolutely not! We are betrothed and soon to be wed!'

"That is the reason I would offer myself. Why would I care otherwise?' smiled Bhoora.

'What if he doesn't prefer you?'

'I doubt he will choose a woman. Given the unfortunate incident of his girlfriend being shot, it is possible that he may exhibit empathy towards women,'

'I shiver at the thought. We shouldn't have agreed to fetch sahib,' suggested Bhoori.

'It was your decision after Jumman withdrew. Are you feeling apprehensive?'

'Yes absolutely! What about you?'

'Who wouldn't feel fear against Sherkhan?'

'Just a little while ago, you were volunteering yourself!'

'I do not wish for it to conclude... I mean, I would never choose Sherkhan's jaws,'

'Even I do not wish for this to be our fate. I desire to start a family with you,' Bhoori said with a bashful smile.

'There is no doubt,'

'Can we talk something else?'

'Shall we rest?'

'No, we should continue moving. We must arrive before sunset.'

'We are almost there. I can see the dam from here.'

'Okay, let's have some water under a shade and then we will move!' suggested Bhoori.

'Umm... you have taken a considerable risk in order to arrive at this location,' Cook remarked.' said Cook.

'We had no alternative. We were determined to inform you of the entire incident,' Bhoora replied.

'It's a pity that Khan won't be here,' sighed Mrs Cook.

'Sherkhan devoured him entirely!' Bhoora exclaimed, widening his eyes.

'What precisely occurred there, Bhoora?' asked Cook.

'I am uncertain of the exact details. I do not know why Khan was at the well. It appears that Sherkhan killed him at the well,'

'Why Sherkhan didn't harm the other man?' asked Mrs Cook.

'He remained behind the closed door. I believe Sherkhan was aware of other man's presence,' replied Bhoora.

'I comprehend that Khan was responsible for shooting the tigress. I have not previously encountered any evidence to suggest that a tiger would pursue humans in order to exact revenge.'

'Yes, it's unbelievable!' said Mrs Cook with fear in her eyes.

'Memsahib! We need to get back before dark,' said Bhoori.

'Let me get the rifle and spare bullets!' said Cook.

'Sahib! Please take whatever is necessary for a night. You might have to stay there,'

'I will come along!' Mrs Cook said.

'It would be dangerous. We need someone to stay here!'

'No, I will come. I will pack dinner and take some water,'

'Yes, there is no water there! I will help you pack,' said Bhoori.

'Untie Shera!'

Shera, the dog wagged his tail seeing Bhoori. She caressed him softly.

'Yes, we would need him!' said Bhoora.

'Where is the caretaker?' asked Cook.

'Hariya seems to have vanished!'

'Blame it on Sherkhan! I believe he has fallen to the ferocious tiger,' sighed Cook.

Prakash, Jumman, and others greeted Cook and Mrs Cook. It was a relief for them in the safety of a gun. Shera, meanwhile, assumed a seated position with his tail tucked between his hind legs.

'Salaam Sahib!' said Jumman respectfully.

'Salaam Jumman! Please close the main door!' replied Cook.

'Long live Sahib!' Prakash expressed his respect.

'Hmm… what exactly happened here? Where is the man who was with Khan?' asked Cook. He was in the room with others.

'Salaam Sahib! I was with Khan sahib,' Gangu said softly.

'Yes, sahib, he is Gangu from our village,' said Jumman. He had closed the main door. The rest house was safely locked. Prakash lightened the lantern that was brought by Mrs Cook.

'Gangu! You are safe now. Sherkhan won't come back. If he tries then he will meet the gun. Please tell me why Khan shot the tigress only,'

'Sahib, I don't know about it. I was on the other tree. Sherkhan ran into the forest after the shot.'

'What happened next?'

'After Sherkhan ran away, Khan sahib signaled me to come down from the tree and he followed suit,' replied Gangu

'Hmm... interesting, go on,'

'Khan sahib wanted to return to the rest house. He had some work at the dam. I came along,'

'I understand you were afraid to go back to the village alone. What happened after that?'

'Sahib! When we were near the rest house, Sherkhan growled. It was unknown to us that Sherkhan had been trailing us throughout our journey,'

'Did you manage to see Sherkhan?'

'No, sahib. We didn't see Sherkhan when we were heading back. It was only upon nearing the rest house that Sherkhan emitted a fierce growl,' explained Gangu.

'What did Khan do?'

'He fired shots in the air! He also shot a few bullets in the bush! But, Sherkhan was nowhere to be seen. However, Sherkhan was silent for a few minutes after the shots,'

'I can't believe Sherkhan followed you,' Mrs Cook expressed surprise.

'What happened after that?'

'Khan and I started running towards the rest house. Sherkhan growled furiously. It was certain that he was following us. We were scared and shaky!'

'Where was Hariya?' asked Cook.

'We didn't see him. He was not here when we reached the rest house. Khan fired shots to unlock the main door.'

'He is still missing!' said Prakash.

'Hmm… there is possibility of him being fallen to Sherkhan. Did Sherkhan try to enter the rest house?'

'Yes, around midnight, he tried to bring down the main door. But it was tough for him. He couldn't manage it,'

'What did Khan do?'

'He was as shaky as me. We remained in the room while Sherkhan threatened us and growled loudly,'

'You should be thankful that Sherkhan didn't bring the main door down!' smiled Jumman.

'Yes, I am thankful to be alive!'

'I understand now. Khan aimed at the tigress and killed her. Subsequently, Sherkhan fled into the forest, but later on, he mustered the courage to return. Upon his return, he observed Khan and Gangu standing beside a tree. Sherkhan, being astute, harbored suspicions that Khan was in possession of a potentially hazardous object, conceivably a firearm. It is plausible that Sherkhan had previously encountered a firearm. As Khan and Gangu proceeded towards the rest house, Sherkhan covertly trailed them.'

'Not a grass moves when maneater walks the forest!' said Bhoora with a sigh.

'But why Khan was killed at the well? What brought him to the well?' Cook raised his eyebrow.

'Water!' said Gangu

'Water?' asked Prakash.

'Sahib requested tea but there was no water in the rest house,' replied Gangu.

'Did Khan go to fetch water?'

'No, it was my fault. He asked me to fetch water from the well. However, I refused. I was afraid of Sherkhan,'

'This is the reason Khan was at the well!' Cook raised his hands.

'But, why didn't he shoot Sherkhan when he ran towards him?' asked Mrs Cook.

'I am as confused as you are, Memsahib! I am not sure why he threw a pot at the tiger,' Gangu expressed surprise.

'He must have hypnotized Khan. We have heard stories about Sherkhan. He hypnotizes men with his fiery eyes,' Jumman suggested.

'Haa… all these are baseless. No animal can hypnotize men!' dismissed the sahib.

'Sherkhan is no animal, sahib. He is a fiery creature!'

'Did you see where Sherkhan went after finishing his meal?'

'Sahib, he kept looking at the main door. I was too afraid and closed the window.'

'What would we do now, sahib?' asked Prakash.

'We will find Sherkhan and bring him down. We can't allow him to hunt men like this.' Cook replied.

'Will you go after him? What would happen to the project?'

'No, I will ask Johnny and Mike to hunt Sherkhan. They are professional hunters!'

'Where are they?'

'They have camped at Kyari village. I will send a runner to them.' Cook smiled. Prakash smiled back.

Banke interrupted his narration briefly.

'Sahib! While Cook sahib sent runners for Johnny and Mike, Sherkhan did something extraordinarily,'

'What did he do?' I raised my eyebrow.

'He moved towards the railways that had just started goods supplies,'

'Do you mean he targeted passengers?'

'No Sir! There was no passenger train in those days for Corbett Park. The railways only carried goods,'

'Did he carry off the guard or a station master like Kima?'

'I will come to it. I am aware of Kima man-eater,'

'Wasn't that extraordinary man-eater?'

'Yes, the lion was ferocious but less as compared to Tsavo!'

'Man-eaters like Tsavio never appeared in wildlife history. They were ferocious, cunning and opportunistic!'

'Sherkhan was no less either, Sahib!'

'I want to know what happened at the station.'

'You will surely know!' Banke smiled at me. I smiled back.

While Cook and others were in discussion, the man arrived on the horse. He was a coolie at the station.

'Is anybody here?' the man shouted.

Cook peered out of the window and signaled for Jumman to open the door.

'Open the door, Jumman!' Cook signaled.

The man entered the room. He was medium-built with brown eyes and a light beard.

'I went to the dam and they told me that I would find Sahib at the rest house,'

'You took a great risk, mate!'

'Sahib! A large tiger had taken an assistant engineer from the railways.' Coolie shared alarming news.

'This tiger seems to be fond of engineers!' Cook made a sarcastic remark.

'Did tiger take any engineer from the dam, sahib?' Coolie widened his eyes.

'Yes, indeed, he has taken our dam engineer! Please forgive me. I meant to say the engineer who works at the dam,' replied Cook with a hesitant smile.'

'How did it happen?' asked Coolie.

'Bhoola will narrate to you the incident. But it happened outside and near the well,'

'Goodness! This is quite alarming!'

'Yes, you have taken a considerable risk by coming here. The tiger must be lurking nearby the railway,' Cook remarked, raising his eyebrow.

'Indeed, he was previously in close proximity to the railway vicinity as we discerned the resonating calls of a tiger. We presumed such occurrences to be customary during this particular season.'

'What precisely happened at the railways?'

'The engineer was inspecting the lights on goods boggy. The tiger jumped from behind when the engineer bent a little,'

'It appears that the tiger had been observing the engineer and waiting for an opportunity,' said Cook.

'What time was it?' asked Prakash.

'Yesterday evening!' the coolie answered.

'Sherkhan had killed the engineer at the rest house just a day prior, which suggests that he had made his way directly to the railways from there,' Cook remarked.

'There is a great possibility that Sherkhan is aware of railways as he was of the rest house,' suggested Bhoora.

'Did he kill any other person before the engineer at the railways?' asked Cook.

'The tiger certainly did not kill anyone else at the railways. But we knew that there was a man-eater in the forest who was preying on runners, poachers, and the villagers,' replied coolie.

'What do we do now, Sahib?' sighed Bhoora.

'Johnny and Mike would take care of Sherkhan. I will send a runner for them,' Cook said.

'Did you find engineer who was taken away?' asked Prakash.

'No, we didn't search for him. But we are sure that he is lying somewhere near the railway forest,' said coolie.

'We will find him!' Cook declared.

'How he will return?' asked Bhoora.

'It would not be advisable for him to go back today, as it is already dark. We will all spend the night here. We will drop him at the railways,'

'I will hitch up the horse!' said Coolie.

'Yes, you can secure him in the verandah.' suggested Cook.

'I will bring Shera inside,' said Bhoora.

'How did the coolie manage to arrive safely without encountering Sherkhan?' asked Prakash.

'Sherkhan must have been preoccupied with the engineer. Otherwise, he would have already disposed of him,'

'Why did he consume two individuals within such a short timeframe?' Prakash asked, displaying a quizzical expression.

'Sherkhan is of considerable size and is likely experiencing hunger. It is important to note that he did not consume Gangu's cow. He has gone without sustenance for a period of two days,' explained Cook.

'How we will drop him?'

'Prakash and Bhoora will walk with Gangu. I will be in the front and coolie at the back,'

'Can I come along?' asked Bhoori.

'No, you and Mrs Cook will walk back to the dam with Jumman and others. Keep Shera in the front!' Cook said.

'I will surely!' Mrs Cook agreed.

'Please listen to me, everybody! I will drop coolie at the railways and Gangu at the village. Prakash and Bhoora will come along. It is imperative that you do not venture alone into the forest and retire to your huts after nightfall. Please ensure that you have relieved yourselves before evening hours.' Cook instructed workers.

Mrs. Cook chuckled and clarified, 'Indeed, he intended for you to refrain from consuming any beverages after nightfall.'

'Now, please lie down in the main room. Memsahib and Bhoori will stay in the bedroom. Bhoora, Prakash, and coolie will take their place along with me in the kitchen.' Cook said.

The forest exuded a sense of tranquility. Sherkhan, on the other hand, was miles away near the railways. The group moved in close proximity, with Cook leading the way. Bhoora, Prakash, and Gangu followed closely behind Cook, while the coolie kept a watchful eye on the rear. Cook initiated a conversation with Gangu, inquiring about his experiences with Sherkhan.

'Gangu! You must be having stories about Sherkhan. Yes, he followed you and Khan. Butthis was not the only thing he did. Tell us about his hunt!' asked Cook.

'Sahib! We were surprised when Sherkhan followed us. We were terrified and it did shake us. This was an unusual behavior as he had never displayed such behavior before. However, we were confined to our huts because of his recent ruthless killing of Abdul Mahawat,'

'Abdul Mahawat,' Bhoora widened his eyes and continued, 'He was a fearless Mahawat and most sought after! It's a shame that Sherkhan didn't spare him.'

'What exactly happened?' Cook inquired.

Gangu replied, 'Abdul Mahawat was indeed fearless, but his cow elephant, Jhumri, abandoned him when he needed her the most.'

'Yes, cow elephants can become terrified of tigers,'

'It was a pleasant afternoon when Abdul and Jhumri ventured into the forest in search of sustenance. Abdul sought food for Jhumri, while berries were gathered for the family's nourishment.'

'I can understand the shortage of food because of Sherkhan. We didn't face it because we were at the dam.' Bhoora said.

'Abdul had climbed a tree, while Jhumri was preoccupied with consuming leaves when Sherkhan stealthily approached them. There was no indication of the tigress's presence. Upon searching for Abdul, only Sherkhan's paw prints were discovered.' Gangu said.

'Why Jhumri was unaware of his presence?' asked Cook.

'Sherkhan possessed a skill for stalking without revealing himself. Although we could sense his presence when he followed us, but we were unable to see him, while he had the advantage of sight. This may explain why Jhumri was unable to detect him.' replied Gangu.

'What exactly happened with them?'

'After collecting a basketful of berries and fruits, Abdul leaped from the tree bark directly to the ground without taking any precautions,'

'I believe there was no need for him to exercise excessive caution, as it was a routine for him,' opined the coolie.

'I disagree. Sherkhan had already stationed men behind closed doors, and all the poachers, runners, and villagers were aware of his presence. Abdul was a bit careless,' countered Bhoora.

'I would not characterize it as carelessness. Perhaps, he had great faith in his instincts and Jhumri's loyalty,' suggested Cook.

'When Jhumri turned towards Abdul to retrieve him, she was taken aback to see Sherkhan standing behind him. Not a leaf stirred when Sherkhan arrived. Only Jhumri's loud noise broke the silence and caused a commotion,' recounted Gangu.

'It must have been a harrowing experience for the unfortunate animal,' remarked the coolie.

'What actions did Abdul take?' inquired Cook.

'Abdul had a premonition of the tiger's presence by observing Jhumri's behavior. Astonishingly, Abdul had an opportunity to turn back,' replied the coolie.

'How can you make such a claim?' questioned Cook.

'When we discovered Abdul, there were no indications of any injuries on his back or back of the neck,' explained the coolie.

'This implies it was a frontal assault!' exclaimed Cook.

'Indeed, there were bite marks on the front of his neck. Abdul's eyes were filled with terror when we found him. Sherkhan pounced on him like a dog would on its owner. Sherkhan knocked Abdul down and killed him,'

'It must have been terrifying for Jhumri,'

'She didn't wait to see what happened to Abdul. She abandoned him and ran towards the village,'

'I won't blame her!' concluded Cook.

'You must have observed the consequences that befell Abdul merely by observing her,' stated the coolie.

'No, she didn't reach the village. We found her in the river. She refused to come out. When Abdul didn't reach the village that night, we initiated the search the following day and found him.'

'Did Sherkhan consume Abdul fully like Khan?'

'No, he didn't eat Abdul. Maybe, he was not hungry. Perhaps, he killed Abdul because of his presence there. Who can say for certain?'

'How can you assert that Sherkhan was not hungry? Did he communicate this to you?' the coolie chuckled.

'We discovered the remains of a buffalo near the location where Abdul was slain. I believe Abdul may have disturbed him during his meal and paid the price.'

'Indeed, it was quite substantial!' Cook sighed.

'What else can you disclose about Sherkhan?'

'Sherkhan is an unrelenting murderer. The day prior to this incident, we ventured into the jungle as a large group to gather Jamun. From the higher branch we saw Sherkhan and his girlfriend,' said Gangu.

'Did they engage in hunting?' inquired Cook.

'Yes, but only Sherkhan. I am unsure of his motivation, but he senselessly killed a large buffalo and its calves,'

'Hmm... there must be some underlying reason!' suggested Bhoora.

'Yes, to impress his girlfriend. He slaughtered them in an attempt to gain her favor,' proposed Cook.

'It is a common behavior among men. Don't we often try to showcase our abilities to impress women?' remarked the coolie.

'Yes, I concur. I have also attempted to impress Bhoori!' chuckled Bhoora.

'Sherkhan even arranged meals for the lady!' added the coolie.

'No, they did not consume the slaughtered animals. As I mentioned, Sherkhan did it solely to impress his girlfriend,' clarified Gangu.

'This particular beast presents a unique challenge. It would be quite an accomplishment to capture him,' stated Cook.

'You will need to approach it in a distinct manner, Sahib. Sherkhan is unlike any other tiger!'

'Diverse circumstances call for varied approaches,' Cook sighed.

The runner apprised Johnny and Mike of Sherkhan and his acts of murder. Johnny and Mike, being seasoned hunters, had recently returned from England with the intention of selling the properties they had acquired during British rule.

'Hello, Mike! It appears we have a potential venture here!'

'Do you truly wish to invest in this place? Will they accept us?'

'No, my friend! I am referring to the notorious maneater.'

'Johnny, we have already hunted numerous tigers and man-eaters. We have had our fair share!'

'Indeed, this situation seems to be somewhat distinct.'

'All predators exhibit similar behavior. They stealthily track their prey and launch surprise attacks from behind,'

'However, Mike, this particular predator pursued the man out of a desire for vengeance. I have never encountered such a phenomenon before,'

'The informant informed us that this man had fatally wounded his girlfriend. It seems that some individuals will go to great lengths to protect their loved ones. Even I would not hesitate to take action against a man, who has caused harm to my own,' Mike chuckled.

'I shall personally confront him,' declared Johnny.

'Has he claimed any other victims?' inquired Mike.

'Yes, he also murdered a railway engineer just a day prior,' Johnny replied.

'Have they managed to locate the perpetrator?'

'No, they have not. It is believed that he may be hiding in the nearby forest,'

'We must evacuate this camp immediately. We must arrive at the destination before nightfall!'

'Cook will meet us at that location!'

'The creature spared the other individual who was an accomplice in illegal activities. What a stroke of good luck!'

'Perhaps he was merely present at the scene or he may not have fired the shot,'

'Regardless! I detest man-eating animals!' smiled Mike. Johnny reciprocated the smile.

'You are now completely safe. Just refrain from entering the forest,' Cook advised Gangu.

'I am very thankful! I wish Khan had dropped me at the village that day. He would have been alive!'

'Sherkhan would have pursued him regardless. If not on that day, he would have eventually killed him. He had his scent!'

'Please remain indoors!' requested Bhoora.

'Indeed, Sherkhan may have moved away from the railway tracks. He possesses your scent, just like Khan's,'

'I am filled with fear, sir! What will we have to eat? We are currently lacking a cow,' Gangu expressed concern.

'I possess a basket brimming with bread and fruits for your sustenance. It will only require a few days to track down Sherkhan. Following that, our routine will resume as usual,' assured Cook.

'Once again, I extend my gratitude, sir!' Gangu expressed his appreciation by folding his hands and bowing.

Cook, Prakash, Bhoora, and Coolie continued their journey towards the railways.

'In light of the circumstances, we must remain exceedingly vigilant,' suggested Cook.

'I am prepared to face Sherkhan!' declared Bhoora, brandishing a sword.

'I am detecting the presence of a predator,' Coolie alerted.

'Indeed, the birds are chirping and the langur has emitted a cry from the highest branch,' Bhoora agreed.

'Hush... remain calm,' Cook advised.

Chaos ensued when a leopard leaped from a nearby branch. The horse of the coolie retreated and Bhoora tumbled to the ground. Prakash, taking Bhoora's sword, ascended the tree, leaving Cook to fend for himself. The leopard showed no interest in them and instead ran towards a group of deer. The deer scattered in all directions in an attempt to save themselves. The leopard seized its meal from the group and climbed to the highest branch. Bhoora joined Prakash in the tree, grasping him by the neck, and they both fell to the ground. Cook intervened and rescued Prakash from Bhoora, restoring peace. The coolie returned once everything had settled. The sword lay unattended, much like Khan's gun. It was just before dusk when they finally arrived at the station.

'Congratulations on your successful arrival, my friend,' exclaimed Johnny as he warmly embraced Cook.

'Indeed, it was by the grace of the Lord,' replied Cook as he shook hands with Mike, 'Have you managed to locate the engineer?

'Yes, he is currently near the tracks,' responded Johnny..

'Have you caught any scent of Sherkhan?' asked Cook.

'I am certain that he is observing us from the bushes. A man-eater such as he never leaves his prey for extended periods of time. I discharged a few rounds,' replied Johnny.

'That was a rather heroic decision,'

'Why is that so?' questioned Johnny.

'You would have been marked by Sherkhan, just like Khan. Sherkhan detests firearms and is no ordinary tiger,' explained Cook. 'What are your plans for Sherkhan?'

'I have summoned a carriage. Mike will be seated inside with a porter," replied Johnny.

'And where will you be hiding?' asked Cook.

'I shall be seated atop the carriage,' laughed Johnny.

'This is highly foolish. It appears that you are dismissing the seriousness of the situation with Sherkhan. Are you following the same path as Kima? Have you forgotten the unfortunate events that occurred with Ryall?'

Bhoora inquired, 'What happened in Kima?'

'Well, there was a man-eating lion in Kima that specifically targeted railway employees. It had already attacked and devoured an assistant station master and a coolie,' explained Cook.

The coolie declared, 'I will confine myself with Cook sahib. I refuse to go anywhere.'

'Yes, the Kima Lion had a preference for railway employees. Ryall happened to arrive in Kima with his companions and expressed an interest in hunting down the Kima lion,' continued the speaker.

Curious, Bhoora asked, 'Could you please provide more details about what transpired?'

'Ryall and his friends took turns in the cabin to hunt down the lion of Kima. However, they neglected to properly secure the cabin door. It was not securely closed. When it was Ryall's turn to be on guard, his friend attempted to wake him up but inadvertently fell asleep. Ryall took some time to awaken. In that moment, the lion entered through the open door and swiftly seized Ryall, as if he were a mere mouse. The lion then escaped through the window of the cabin with Ryall,' recounted the speaker.

'Isn't it horrific?' inquired the coolie.

'Yes, it certainly was. I find it difficult to believe that Johnny is pursuing the same course of action.'

'No, I am not following the same plan. Mike will be seated in the carriage with a coolie, ensuring that the doors are securely locked. From the window, they will aim for Sherkhan. I, on the other hand, will be perched atop the large tree adjacent to the track where the engineer is lying. Sherkhan will approach Mike from behind, and I will shoot him from the tree.'

'But won't Sherkhan notice you on the tree?'

'No, there will be no machaan. I will be alone on the tree.'

'Well, it appears to be a favorable plan, but it carries a significant amount of risk. How do you propose to navigate in the darkness?'

'There will be a lantern inside the carriage. Sherkhan will be visible. In fact, I want Mike and Coolie to be visible as well. Furthermore, it would be impossible for Sherkhan to enter the securely locked carriage.'

Cook glanced at Bhoora. Prakash also found the explanation unconvincing. Bhoora looked at Prakash, who returned the gaze. They were uncertain about Johnny's decision.

'Sir, I still have concerns,' Bhoora expressed. At that moment, they all heard a loud growl emanating from the forest. Sherkhan made his presence known. Mike swiftly climbed onto the carriage with his rifle strapped to his back. Cook, Prakash, Coolie, and Bhoora entered the carriage and locked it. Johnny joined Mike on the roof. Without hesitation, Johnny seized the rifle from Mike and fired shots.

'This is remarkable!' exclaimed Prakash.

'I told you these men fear no one. Sherkhan's reign is coming to an end!' declared Cook.'

'I have doubts that Sherkhan will be intimidated by this. Despite Khan firing shots at him, Sherkhan persisted and ultimately killed him,' said Prakash.

Banke then paused. 'Sir, it was unforeseeable that Sherkhan had already set his sights on his target that evening and was merely waiting for the opportune moment.'

'Are you suggesting that Sherkhan had premeditated his actions?'

Banke replied, 'Indeed, sir. The rifle in his possession aided him in his plan. Johnny was the one who fired the shots, and Sherkhan had control over Johnny and his weapon.'

'Ah, so Sherkhan perceived Johnny as the threat, not Mike. Did he spare Mike like Gangu did?'

Banke said with a smile, 'We will find it out.'

Banke then resumed the narration,

'Your actions are commendable, Johnny,' Cook stated.

'As a team, we have established a reputation for such bravery, have we not?'

'Before we assume our positions, let us partake in a beverage.'

'I suggest we retire to the cloakroom, where we can remain in close proximity in the event of any unforeseen circumstances,' Cook proposed.

Johnny interjected, 'This rifle requires no assistance. You need only wait for the sound of Sherkhan's cries of agony.'

Bhoora murmured, 'I highly doubt Sherkhan would cry.'

'Silence!' Cook snapped at Bhoora. Johnny erupted in laughter.

In the cloakroom, Bhoora posed a question, 'Sir, how did the phenomenon of man-eaters come to be? Who was the earliest recorded maneater?'

'I am not acquainted with a multitude of narratives; however, I shall proceed to recount a tale that elucidates the evolution of the initial man-eating tiger.'

'It is believed that in the distant past, there was a proprietor known as a "bunya" who operated a small daily needs store in the village. The bunya would frequently travel to the city to procure goods to sell in his shop. However, on one occasion, a large tiger emerged from the nearby forest and began to prey on the livestock of the village, causing great distress to the local community. The tiger would often block the road connecting the village to the city, preventing travelers from passing through. As a result, the bunya's business suffered significant losses, and he sought the counsel of an elderly priest residing in a neighboring village. The priest provided the bunya with a powder, instructing him to keep it in his pocket and consume it if he encountered the tiger. Upon ingestion, the bunya would transform into a tiger and could either defeat or intimidate the other tiger. Afterward, the bunya would need to consume a small amount of the powder to revert to his human form.'

'Oh! It's a compelling story. I never heard it.'Bhoora said with a nervous smile.

'Once, Bunya and his wife were traveling in their carriage when they encountered a tiger on the road. In response, Bunya retrieved a vial of powder from his pocket and proceeded to elucidate the situation to his wife. It was evident that the woman was overcome with fear. Bunya then handed her a pouch containing the remaining powder and implored her to keep it in her possession. He assured her that upon his return, he would ingest the remaining powder in order to revert back to his human form.'

'I would have run back, no matter what. It was brave of that woman to stay there. What happened after that?'

'The bunya distanced itself a few meters away from the woman and ingested the powder, with the intention of avoiding any distress to the unfortunate wife. Subsequently, the bunya transformed into the likeness of a substantial tiger and pursued another tiger. The entire jungle bore witness to the bone-chilling roars emitted by the colossal felines engaged in combat. Ultimately, the tiger bunya emerged victorious and subsequently reunited with his spouse.'

'The wife would have passed out seeing a large tiger in front of her.'

'No, she did not. Upon encountering a large tiger directly in front of her, the woman emitted a piercing scream and hastily fled toward the nearby village. In the midst of her panic, the powder she held in her hand inadvertently slipped into the small stream of water that flowed down from the gentle hill. Consequently, the tiger known as Bunya found himself devoid of the transformative powder that would have restored him to his human form. Thus, he was condemned to forever inhabit the body of a tiger. Consumed by anguish, he tragically took the life of his wife before vanishing into the depths of the forest, forever remaining a tiger. Subsequently, possessing the physical form of a tiger but the cognitive abilities of a human, he acquired an intimate understanding of human behavior. This newfound knowledge led him to prey upon humans, ultimately transforming him into a man-eating creature. Thus, the first man-eating tiger emerged, passing down its taste for human flesh through subsequent generations.' Cook concluded the narrative.

The evening was enveloped in complete darkness, devoid of any audible sounds. The prevailing silence was remarkably profound, evoking an eerie atmosphere. The biting cold compelled Cook and his companions to hastily seek shelter within the cloakroom. Johnny relied on the illumination provided by his torch beam and the lantern within the cabin. Mike was depicted as potential prey for Sherkhan, yet he possessed a firearm and vigilantly scanned his surroundings. Adjacent to the vicinity, a steady stream flowed, devoid of any elephants partaking in a refreshing bath. The prevailing stillness was deeply unsettling. Sherkhan had stealthily dragged the engineer through the dense foliage and consumed his meal in close proximity to the railway track. Such behavior was highly unusual. Indeed, Sherkhan himself was an enigmatic and peculiar creature, was he not?

The presence of jungle fowl or peafowl, which could have served as evidence of Sherkhan, was noticeably absent. The customary chorus of crickets was conspicuously absent as well. One might question why the crickets would fear the man-eater, as it seemed illogical. Nevertheless, Sherkhan himself exhibited no fear towards anyone. He approached the bogie cautiously, but always from a position behind it. He was fully aware of Johnny's presence in the tree, yet he refrained from roaring or making any noise.

Cook and the others displayed great patience as they awaited the unfolding events. From the thicket, Sherkhan observed the prey and Johnny with a commanding presence. Sherkhan exhibited no interest in Mike or the bogie, as his sole focus was fixed upon Johnny. Perched on his haunches, Sherkhan's impending attack was inevitable. At any moment, he would swiftly ascend and ruthlessly tear Johnny apart with his sharp claws. The tree trembled as Johnny attempted to adjust his sitting position. Given the tree's size, his efforts to reposition himself only served to exacerbate his predicament.

Banke interjected, 'Sir, despite being a professional hunter, Johnny was unaware of the fact that a tiger could pounce from the fallen tree nearby.'

'I am unable to comprehend it,'

'Sir, it has been observed that tigers possess the ability to leap up to a maximum height of ten feet from the ground. In the specific case of Johnny, he was positioned an additional five feet above ground level. It has been stated by the esteemed Corbett that tigers are capable of ascending up to thirty feet in order to procure their sustenance.'

'However, why do they not engage in this activity frequently?'

'Climbing is not the issue; rather, the challenge lies in descending.'

'In close proximity, there was a fallen tree. Johnny was observing the bogie, while Mike had a panoramic view, although the night was shrouded in darkness. Sherkhan, concealed in the undergrowth remained undetectable. Utilizing the fallen tree as a prop, Sherkhan executed a tremendous leap, swiftly seizing Johnny as if he were a mere mouse. The boastful hunter's fate was sealed.'

'Uff... that was truly unbelievable.'

'Indeed, it was!' Banke responded with a smile. He proceeded to elaborate.

'Sir, I believe Khan Sahib sacrificed himself so that you could assist in eliminating Sherkhan.'

'I find it difficult to believe.' Cook replied.

'I don't understand why he threw a pot at Sherkhan instead of firing a shot,'

'Do you believe that Sherkhan has the ability to hypnotize his victims?'

'He certainly hypnotized Khan Sahib. Let us observe if he can do the same to Johnny.'

'Sahib, the Kima lion undeniably hypnotized Ryall sahib. He presented himself as the bait, and the lion graciously accepted.'

'Furthermore, he positioned himself on the back of Ryall's companion to reach him. He stealthily entered through the unlatched door and exited through the open window. What a grave mistake!'

'I would classify it as carelessness.'

The silence was abruptly shattered by a loud growl, followed by a piercing shriek.

'It is Johnny! I am certain it is his voice. It is sharp and cacophonous.'

'It appears that Sherkhan has found his meal,' the coolie said, his voice trembling.

Bhoora said, 'The offer was extended and he graciously accepted it.'

'He was a courageous young man! Who would willingly put themselves in harm's way? I feel sorry for him,' Cook lamented.

'Should we venture outside to gather more information?' Prakash suggested.

'Would you like to partake in a meal?' Cook inquired, pausing momentarily. He proceeded to open the small window in order to observe the ongoing events.

There existed a multitude of fireflies gracefully fluttering in various directions. They emitted a radiant glow amidst the obscurity. Sherkhan had disrupted their tranquility, causing the fireflies to exhibit their nightly exhibition of vibrant illuminations. The prevailing silence was uninterrupted by any other auditory stimuli. The forest appeared to be devoid of any wildlife, with the absence of galloping deer or the calls of nocturnal birds. However, Cook discerned the thumping sound of Sherkhan's approach towards the cloak room. An eerie stillness enveloped the surroundings. Cook promptly raised his Winchester rifle to his shoulder and activated the torch button, projecting its beam through the window. He observed a pair of malevolent eyes that possessed a reddish hue. Sherkhan, positioned on his hind legs akin to a canine, proceeded to moisten his lips. The crimson tongue glided across his slightly parted mouth. Sherkhan was illuminated by the light, which shone intensely into his eyes. Cook became entranced, rendering him speechless. Sherkhan rose to his feet, emitted a menacing growl, pivoted, and departed. He displayed no interest in Cook, as his intended prey was Johnny, whom he approached with a gentle demeanor. Cook extinguished the torch and rested his head upon his knees. Although Cook harbored anger, he was also consumed by fear. He was unwilling to jeopardize anyone's life. Prakash and Bhoora remained silent, withholding their thoughts. Coolie had succumbed to slumber, overwhelmed by fear. Suddenly, a deafening roar emanated from the depths of the jungle. It appeared that Sherkhan was voraciously consuming his meal. He harbored no fear of torches, firearms, or any human being. In fact, he feared no living creature. At midday, they emerged from their secure concealment. Cook grasped a rifle firmly within his hands, while Prakash and Bhoora trailed closely behind. Bhoora, in turn, brandished a sword in his hands.

'Sir, let us return! We should wait for the others,' Bhoora suggested.

'No one will come, Bhoora. Do you truly believe that the villagers would venture out of their huts?'

'Ms. Cook may come looking for you,'

'Why would she search? She knows that I am capable of handling the tiger!'

'Are you, Sir?' Cook stared sharply at Bhoora. Bhoora lowered his gaze.

They discovered a horrifying scene at the carriage. The rifle lay unattended. The surroundings were eerily quiet. No animal or bird had made its presence known through sight or sound. The banyan tree was large and provided ample hiding places. Cook nervously plucked several handfuls of tough grass stems. He crouched down and then sat on his haunches, attempting to remain completely still. Nevertheless, he was unable to sustain his current position for an extended period of time due to the onset of pain in his ankle and numbness in his leg muscles. Consequently, they exercised heightened vigilance in observing the surrounding jungle, not only in front but also on both sides and behind, in order to safeguard against any potential attack. Upon discovering traces of blood and the presence of a knife, they proceeded cautiously, advancing stealthily until they encountered the path where the large animal had traversed through the tall grass. At this point, Cook instinctively took a step back and signaled for the others to retreat.

'Sherkhan has taken Johnny to the stream,' Cook whispered discreetly.

'Should we pursue them?'

'I lack the fortitude to engage in a confrontation. Let us instead attend to Mike and Coolie.'

Mike trembled, anxiously peering out the window with an impassive gaze. Coolie remained unconscious. Cook attempted to pacify Mike, but his efforts proved futile.

'Please conduct appropriately, Mike,' Cook admonished as he splashed water onto his face.

Mike remained stoic, eliciting a comment from Bhoora that he had a 'stone face.' Cook observed that Johnny had likely been taken without resistance, as evidenced by the wine bottle left on the ground.

'He must be in a state of drowsiness,' Cook surmised.

Bemoaning the situation, Bhoora remarked that it was "insane," to which Cook replied that it had been "invited." Requesting that the window be closed, Cook was asked if he would take a shot at Sherkhan.

'I have already expressed my lack of courage to face Sherkhan,' Cook replied, his nervousness palpable to Bhoora.

'It would be dangerous to confront the man-eater.' said Bhoora.

The primary peril they faced resided in the direction Johnny had been taken. They promptly secured the bogie and patiently awaited further developments. It would be inaccurate to label them as cowards. Evidently, they were reluctant to become entangled with Sherkhan. There was no doubt that he was present, and they were unwilling to take any chances. The cook activated the flashlight. The man-eater was nowhere to be found. They settled in to spend the night in the bogie. It would have been hazardous to approach the cloak room with the senseless Mike and unconscious coolie. The night would be a lengthy and potentially eventful watch. Cook was drowsy, as were the others.

The evening transpired uneventfully, with no notable occurrences. Mike maintained an unwavering gaze, refraining from blinking or speaking. Suddenly, Cook observed the tall grass swaying violently, without any prior indication. This was followed by a deafening roar emitted by Sherkhan. Overwhelmed with fear, Cook switched on the flashlight, his hands trembling uncontrollably. Bhoora and Prakash assumed a low position, seeking safety. Sherkhan, consumed by anger, continued to unleash a series of ferocious roars. Cook positioned himself in the direction from which Sherkhan was roaring, his fingers poised on the knob. The beast began to encircle them, emitting menacing snarls and roars. It became a battle of nerves, as the tiger neither charged nor retreated.

'Do not act so recklessly,' Prakash cautioned.

However, Cook proceeded to discharge the firearm. The impact on Sherkhan was significant, as he lacked the courage to charge forward and instead retreated. Sherkhan may have sensed the difficulty in attacking the bogie. Tigers exhibit great caution when returning to their prey. Nevertheless, Sherkhan carried the food to the stream, which was an unusual behavior for him to visit the bogie for Cook and others. It could have been an act of aggression.

'Did you make eye contact with him, sir?'

'I now believe I may have been hypnotized!' said Cook.

Coolie regained consciousness only briefly.

'Sir, this has been the most dreadful night of my life,' Bhoora expressed.

'It has not been any different for me,' Cook shrugged his shoulders.

Sherkhan consumed Johnny entirely and emitted a resounding roar as he retreated back into the depths of the jungle. They patiently awaited the arrival of the sun. It was a luminous afternoon when they discerned the familiar voice. Mrs. Cook materialized with a complete entourage. She had previously pledged to embark on a search after a span of two days.

'Have you had the opportunity to encounter Sherkhan?' asked Cook.

Mrs. Cook smiled and replied, "We are alive, aren't we? However, the jungle was remarkably silent. Where is Johnny? Why are Mike and Coolie unconscious?' She raised an eyebrow inquisitively.

'They have been in this state for two days!'

'There is blood on the grass. What precisely transpired here? Why don't you inform me of Johnny's whereabouts?' Mrs. Cook bombarded with numerous questions.

'Um... I...,' Cook struggled to articulate.

'That belongs to Johnny!' Bhoora pointed at the blood.

'Oh my... I mean...' Mrs. Cook brought her hands to her head.

'Yes, Sherkhan bears the responsibility for this.'

'Where is Johnny?'

'He is positioned in close proximity to the stream. It is possible that we may not discover anything!'

'Why did you refrain from shooting?' Mrs. Cook exclaimed with great intensity.

'I was unable to do so as I lacked the necessary courage. He possesses the ability to hypnotize you!' Cook shouted.

'Let us retrieve Johnny promptly!' Mrs. Cook gestured to the workers.

The dogs vocalized in an unusual fashion, causing some individuals to express their unease. The search and rescue team carefully placed Johnny inside the sack, while Mike and coolie were secured onto the horse's back. It took several days for everyone to return to their usual state.

The days passed uneventfully, and work commenced at the dam in its customary manner. The newly appointed engineer opted for an alternative route via Kathgodam to reach the dam. Cook and Mrs. Cook made the decision to remain in India and politely declined the opportunity to relocate to England. Mike returned with an expressionless gaze, seemingly affected by his experiences. It is believed that the jungle spirits safeguard the man-eating creatures and possess an uncanny ability to eavesdrop on conversations and discern human thoughts. As twilight approached, Bhoora and Bhoori retraced their familiar path to return to the village.

'Let's get married!' suggested Bhoori.

'We will talk about it when we reach home,' replied Bhoora.

Bhoori expressed her desire to enter into matrimony.

'Why did you choose this particular route? Is it not fraught with peril?'

'Indeed, it does pose a certain level of risk, but the alternative path was considerably longer. Furthermore, the evening has only recently commenced, and...'

'And there could be Sherkhan behind a bush!' laughed Bhoori.

'Conceivably, there may be a lurking danger, such as the presence of Sherkhan concealed within a thicket!' Bhoora chuckled.

'You are attempting to instill fear within me. However, it has been a month since he last engaged in hunting. It is possible that he has relocated to a different area.'

'Predators of this nature seldom abandon their territory.'

'Nevertheless, there have been no reported sightings. Otherwise...' At that precise moment, the Langur watchman sounded the alarm before dusk had descended. The distressing and piercing cry of 'Ha..ah! Harr! Harr!' resonated through the air. This served as a warning to the couple, causing them to freeze in their tracks. The tiger confirmed his presence with a resounding roar, 'Aoongh! Aaoongh!'

A profound silence descended thereafter. Bhoora meticulously surveyed the surrounding foliage and trees, his face drenched in perspiration. Bhoori clung to Bhoora, trembling with fear. The silence was eerie, almost palpable. Bhoora caught sight of the tiger's menacing eyes as it leaped upon Bhoori from the tall grass. Sherkhan seized her by the neck. Bhoora remained motionless, incredulously observing Bhoori. She wept silently, unable to utter a single word. Bhoora locked eyes with Sherkhan, becoming entranced. The deafening roar of Sherkhan reverberated through the dam, catching everyone off guard. The Cook and Mrs. Cook experienced an inexplicable restlessness. Sherkhan began to growl ferociously.

'It appears to be Sherkhan who may have perpetrated the assault on the couple, as they had recently mentioned their intention to travel to the village,' Cook cleared.

'Indeed, Sahib, this individual is Sherkhan,' affirmed Jumman.

'Retrieve the rifle, as I have done,' Mrs. Cook commanded, fearlessly mounting her horse and galloping to the aid of the couple.

'Sahib, please assist in rescuing Bhoora and Bhoori. It is possible that they may have encountered Sherkhan before reaching the village,' Prakash implored.

The Cook followed the trail, and they discovered Bhoora with an expressionless face. Bhoori was lying face down, appearing serene. Sherkhan had not harmed her. Bhoora had bravely confronted Sherkhan with his sword. It seemed that Bhoori would soon regain consciousness.

'Bhoora! I can detect the presence of Sherkhan!' Cook exclaimed. Bhoora remained silent but glanced at Cook.

'I will fire the shots,' Mrs. Cook declared.

'It is futile. No shots can inflict harm upon him,' Bhoora cried out loudly.

'Did Sherkhan pursue you?'

'I cannot confirm, Sahib...' Bhoora cried out once more.

'In which direction did he go?'

'I am uncertain of the situation. She displayed a cheerful demeanor. We were discussing the prospect of marriage. Sherkhan attacked without provocation.'

Mrs. Cook discharged shots into the air and surrounding foliage. This time, the bullet struck Sherkhan, causing him to emit a loud roar of agony. She had wounded Sherkhan. Although he retreated momentarily, it is likely that he will return. Sherkhan viewed Bhoori as mere prey, and his anger will drive him to return.

'What course of action do you propose for dealing with Sherkhan?' Mrs. Cook whispered.

'We must apprehend him this time. We must take a calculated risk,' Cook suggested.

'We must devise a plan to hunt down Sherkhan,' Mrs. Cook added.

'We cannot leave Bhoora alone. Should we abandon Bhoori...'

'I will remain with her,' Bhoora declared loudly.

'Yes, but you will not remain on the ground. You will be with me up in a tree,' Cook stated.

'But I insist on staying!' Mrs. Cook exclaimed.

'Are you out of your mind?' Cook mocked.

'Is it possible to observe the presence of that banyan tree? It possesses a substantial hollow aperture suitable for concealing an individual. I shall position myself within it,' Mrs. Cook conveyed.

'I am adamantly opposed to assuming such a perilous endeavor!'

'We must take the risk at hand. The presence of Sherkhan has become unbearable. It is imperative that we immobilize him. You and Bhoori shall position yourselves on the tree, without the need for concealment. Sherkhan will approach both of you, unaware of my presence. I will then seize the opportunity to neutralize him.' Mrs. Cook proposed.

'Let us not waste any time!' Cook exclaimed. True to form, Sherkhan materialized without warning. He viciously grabbed Bhoori's leg and observed Bhoora and Cook from the ground. This was an unsettling sight for Bhoora, who promptly leaped down from the tree and confronted Sherkhan.

'Please refrain from such foolish behavior, Bhoora...,' Cook shouted sternly from his perch in the tree.

'This act is intended for Bhoori,' Bhoora declared as he hurled a knife at Sherkhan, striking him and causing blood to flow rapidly. Sherkhan bellowed in agony and retaliated by slashing Bhoora's neck, rendering him incapacitated.

'This is for Johnny,' Cook declared as he aimed his firearm at Sherkhan and pulled the trigger. However, Sherkhan was swift in his movements and managed to evade the shot, subsequently bringing Cook down with him and rendering the rifle useless.

'Hey...,' Mrs. Cook emptied the rifle as she emerged from the banyan tree, leaving Sherkhan in a state of disbelief.

'Sahib, Sherkhan was not anticipating the presence of Mrs. Cook,' Banke exclaimed, taken aback.

'Indeed, it was a courageous act for Mrs. Cook to conceal herself in the banyan tree,' I agreed.

'Mrs. Cook proceeded to discharge her firearm at Sherkhan, striking him in the nose and neck with her bullets.'

Sherkhan exhibited an atypical behavior for tigers as he displayed a tendency to trail behind humans. Even after Khan, he did not alter his habits and continued to follow Bhoora and Bhoori. This behavior instilled terror and fear among those who encountered him. Following the gunshots, the jungle fell into an eerie silence. Cook, filled with apprehension, worried that Sherkhan might unexpectedly recover from his injuries.

'It's all over,' Mrs. Cook declared with a smile, glancing at her husband. However, Cook's countenance remained devoid of any joy as he was consumed by fear. He was unable to utter a single word, his gaze fixed upon Mrs. Cook with trepidation. Mrs. Cook turned around to catch a glimpse of the tigress, Sherkhan's companion, who sought vengeance.

www.ingramcontent.com/pod-product-compliance
Lightning Source LLC
LaVergne TN
LVHW091134180726
843490LV00008B/2972